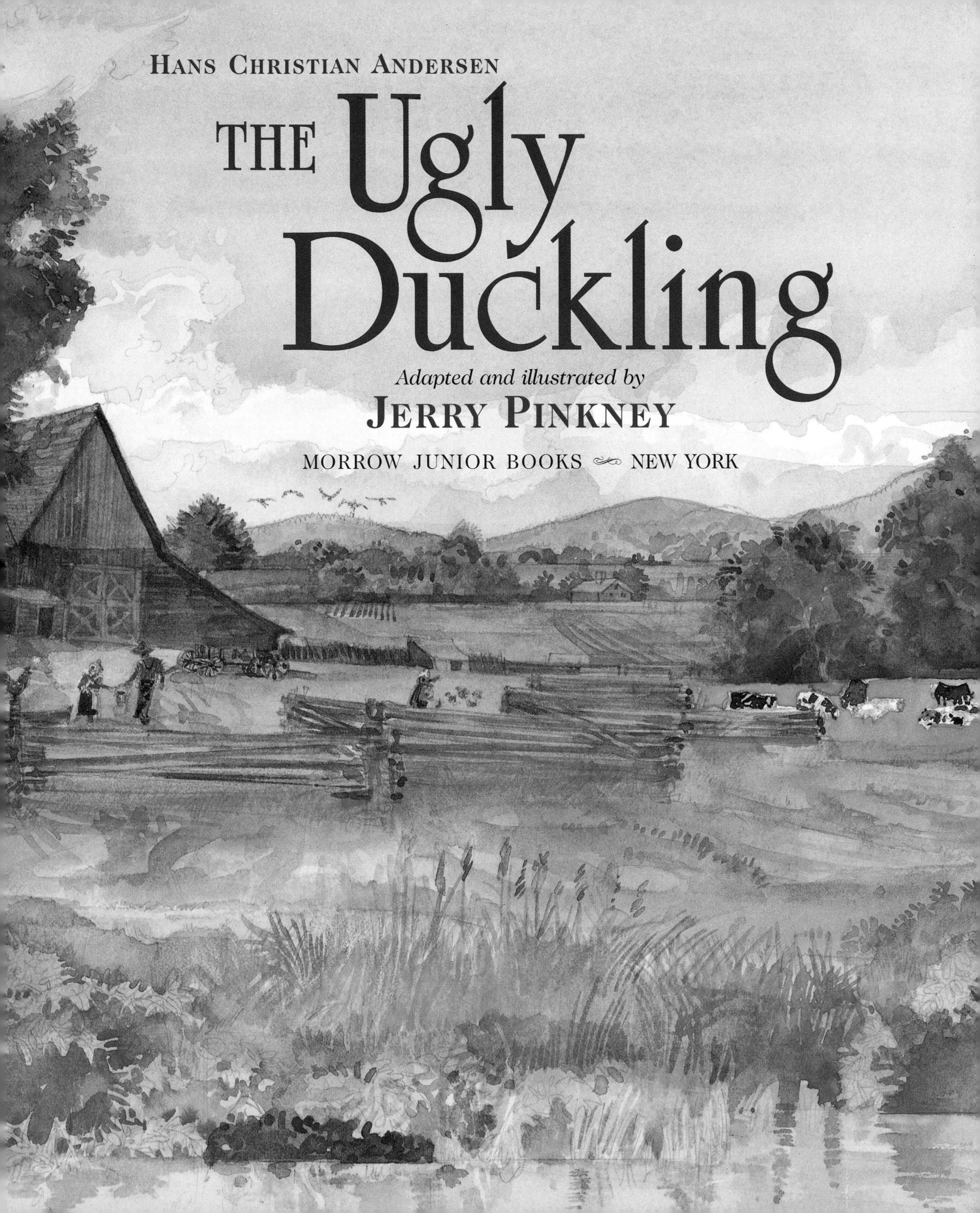

HANS CHRISTIAN ANDERSEN

THE Ugly Duckling

Adapted and illustrated by

JERRY PINKNEY

MORROW JUNIOR BOOKS ∽ NEW YORK

Text adapted from *The Yellow Fairy Book,* compiled by Andrew Lang, and *Andersen's Fairy Tales*
(originally published as *Faery Tales from Hans Andersen*)

Watercolors were used for the full-color illustrations.
The text type is 14-point Caslon 224.

Published by Morrow Junior Books
a division of William Morrow and Company, Inc.
1350 Avenue of the Americas, New York, NY 10019
www.williammorrow.com

Printed in the United States of America.

5 7 9 10 8 6

Library of Congress Cataloging-in-Publication Data
Pinkney, Jerry.
The ugly duckling / Hans Christian Andersen; adapted and illustrated by Jerry Pinkney.
p. cm.
Summary: An ugly duckling spends an unhappy year ostracized by the other animals before he grows into a beautiful swan.
ISBN 0-688-15932-X (trade)—ISBN 0-688-15933-8 (library)
[1. Fairy tales.] I. Andersen, H. C. (Hans Christian), 1805–1875. II. Title.
PZ8.P575Ug 1999 [E]—dc21 98-23604 CIP AC

In appreciation of the wonders of nature
and the gift of time-honored stories
—J.P.

It was summer, and the pond was alive with the music and color of life. Dragonflies danced to and fro, and frogs splashed in and out at the water's edge. Below the surface fish swam together in harmony, while birds swooped through the air above. And all around a gentle breeze rustled the tall grasses that grew nearby.

There, secluded among the grasses, a duck was sitting on six eggs. Five of the eggs were small, but the sixth was oddly shaped and much larger than the others. The duck was puzzled about that egg and how it came to be so different from the rest. But she did not worry herself about it much—she just took care that the big egg was as warm as the rest.

This was the first set of eggs that the duck had ever laid, and she was very pleased and proud. One day, when she saw tiny cracks on two of them, she drew the eggs closer to one another and didn't move for the rest of that day. She sat steadily on the nest for a whole night. Before the sun rose, the five little eggs were empty, and five pairs of eyes were gazing out upon the green world.

"I suppose you are all here now?" said the mother as she stood up. "No, I have not got you all yet! The biggest egg is still there. How long is it going to take?" She settled herself on the nest again.

The day wore on, and the big egg showed no signs of cracking. But all through that day and the next she sat, giving up even her morning bath for fear that a blast of cold might strike the big egg. In the evening she thought she saw a tiny crack in the shell, and she was so excited that she could hardly sleep all night.

With the first streaks of light she felt something stirring under her. Soon a big awkward bird tumbled out of the egg headfirst.

"Cheep, cheep!" cried the young one.

The mother looked with surprise at his long neck and dull color. That is a monstrous big duckling, she said to herself. None of the others looked like that. Can he be a turkey chick? Well, we shall soon find out, she thought, as he and the five furry little balls followed her to the water.

"Did you ever see anything quite as ugly as that great creature?" one of the ducks in the yard taunted as the family walked by.

"He is a disgrace to any brood," another agreed. "I shall go and chase him out!" And he ran to the big duckling and bit his neck.

"Leave him alone," the duckling's mother said fiercely. "He is doing no harm."

"No, but he is so ugly that no one can put up with him," answered the stranger, and the poor duckling drooped his head.

"He may not be quite as handsome as the others," his mother answered, comforting him, "but he is tall and very strong. I am sure he will make his way in the world as well as anybody."

But as time went by, matters grew worse. The poor duckling was chased by all of them, even his brothers and sisters. The ducks bit him, the hens pecked him, and the girl who fed them kicked him aside. At last he could bear it no longer, and one night, when the ducks and hens were still asleep, he stole away. By dawn he had reached a grassy moor, full of soft marshy places.

It was peaceful there, and the duckling wished that he might stay forever, away from everyone, until—

Bang! Bang!

At the sound of the gun whole flocks of wild geese flew up from the rushes. Sportsmen lay hidden around the marsh, and some even sat on the branches of trees that overhung the water. For a few long minutes the firing continued.

Luckily the duckling could not fly, and he floundered along through the water till he could hide himself among some tall ferns. But hunting dogs were wandering about in the swamp—*splash! splash!*—and just at that moment a frightful dog appeared beside him. His tongue hung right out of his mouth, and his eyes glared wickedly. The duckling grew cold with terror and tried to hide his head beneath his little wings.

The dog opened his great chasm of a mouth close to the duckling, showed his sharp teeth, and then—*splash!*—went on without touching him.

I am too ugly even for a dog to eat, the duckling thought. Well, that is a blessing. But I will never go near this pool again—*never!*

And so the duckling marched on bravely all day long until he reached a small cottage. The door had fallen off one hinge and hung so crookedly that he could creep into the house through the crack. He lay down there, exhausted, and spent the entire night in peace.

Now, in the cottage dwelt an old woman, her cat, and a hen, and the next morning the duckling awoke to the sight of all three looming over him.

"What on earth is that?" said the old woman, whose sight was not good.

"Can you lay eggs?" asked the hen. The trembling duckling shook his head.

"Can you ruffle your fur when you are angry, or purr when you are pleased?" asked the cat. But the duckling had to admit that he could do nothing but swim.

"So, it can neither lay eggs nor purr," said the hen.

"What should we do with it?" cried the cat.

"Oh, you are all talking nonsense," replied the old woman. "We will let it stay for a bit, for I am sure we will see some eggs from the creature soon enough."

The duckling remained for three weeks, but he laid not a single egg. Before long he grew restless, for he wanted more than anything to have a swim.

"What is the matter?" asked the hen.

"I am so longing to float on the water again," said the duckling. "You can't imagine how delicious it is to feel it rushing over your head when you dive straight to the bottom."

"I don't think I would enjoy it," replied the hen doubtfully. And the cat agreed there was nothing she would hate so much.

"Haven't you lived in this warm room and in our company long enough to have learned to do anything useful?" said the hen.

"I suppose not," said the duckling. "I think I must go back into the wide world."

The cat and the hen answered shortly, "Very well then, go." And they turned their backs on him before he could even say good-bye.

So the duckling left his friends. He was sad, but he could not help feeling a thrill of joy when he was out in the air and swimming in the water once more.

Now the autumn came. The leaves in the woods turned yellow and brown, and the wind took hold of them and they danced about. The clouds hung heavy with snow and hail. Then the snow began to fall, and to the duckling's bewilderment, the river started to turn hard and slippery.

One day he heard a sound of whirring wings, and up in the air he saw a flock of birds flying high. They were as bright as the snow that had fallen during the night, and their long necks were stretched southward. Oh, if only he could go with them! But what sort of companion could he be to those beautiful beings?

Every morning it grew colder and colder, and the duckling had to swim about in the water to keep it from freezing. At last, during one bitter night, his legs moved so slowly that the ice crept closer and closer. When the morning light broke, he was caught fast.

By good fortune a man was crossing the river and saw what had happened. He stamped the ice so hard that it broke, and then he picked up the duckling and tucked him under his sheepskin coat, where the little bird's frozen bones began to thaw.

The man took the bird to his children, who gave him warm food to eat and put him in a box by the fire. They were kind children and wanted to play with him, but the poor duckling had never played in his life. He thought they wanted to tease him, and so he flew, terrified at the noise and confusion, right out the door.

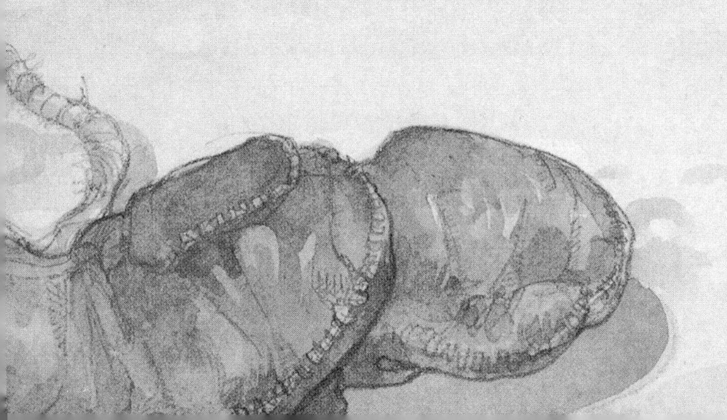

The rest of the winter was miserable, and the duckling never had enough to eat. But finally the earth became softer, and tender young plants poked through. When the duckling stood up one day, he raised his wings and stretched them in the warmth of the sun. He flapped them once, and then again and again, with a strength he had never felt before.

Just in front of him he saw a flock of the same beautiful birds he had seen in the sky so many months ago. One by one he watched them step into the stream, with feathers rustling, and then float quietly upon the water as if they were part of it.

I will follow them, thought the duckling. *I would rather be killed by them than suffer any more cold and hunger and cruelty.*

And stretching out his wings, he lifted himself into the air to fly down to the water.

Oh, how glorious it felt to be rushing through the air, wheeling first one way and then another. He had never thought flying could be like this!

When he reached the water, some of the younger birds swam out to meet him with cries of welcome, which the duckling hardly understood. "I don't know why I was hatched. I am the ugliest duckling ever to live," he said to them. He bowed his head and looked down into the water.

Reflected in the still pool he saw many graceful shapes, with long necks and golden bills. Without thinking, he looked for his dull feathers and awkward, skinny neck. But no such thing was there. Instead, he beheld beneath him a beautiful swan!

“The new one is the best,” said the children when they came down from the village nearby to feed the swans. “His feathers and his beak are the brightest of all.”

And when he heard that, the swan knew that it was worth having undergone all the suffering and loneliness that he had. Otherwise, he would never have known what it was to be really happy.

The lilacs bent their boughs down to the water before him, and the bright sun was warm and cheering. He rustled his feathers and raised his slender neck aloft, saying with pure joy in his heart, “I never dreamed of such peace.”